For my wife, D[...]
my children,
Yannik, Miro, Nina, and Sophie;
and everyone else
who has accompanied me day by day
through the last sixty years

Marcus Pfister was born in Bern, Switzerland. After studying at the Art School of Bern, he apprenticed as a graphic designer and worked in an advertising agency before becoming self-employed in 1984. His debut picture book, *The Sleepy Owl,* was published by NorthSouth in 1986, but his big breakthrough came six years later with *The Rainbow Fish.* Today, Marcus has illustrated over 65 books, which have been translated into more than 60 languages and received countless international awards. He lives with his wife, Debora, and his children in Bern.

Copyright © 2021 by NordSüd Verlag AG, CH-8050 Zürich, Switzerland.
First published in Switzerland under the title *Franz-Ferdinand will tanzen*.
English translation copyright © 2021 by NorthSouth Books Inc., New York 10016.
Translated by David Henry Wilson.

First published in the United States, Great Britain, Canada, Australia, and New Zealand in 2021
by NorthSouth Books Inc., an imprint of NordSüd Verlag AG, CH-8050 Zürich, Switzerland.

Distributed in the United States by NorthSouth Books Inc., New York 10016.
Library of Congress Cataloging-in-Publication Data is available.
ISBN: 978-0-7358-4469-8
Printed in Latvia on FSC-paper from responsible sources
1 3 5 7 9 • 10 8 6 4 2
www.northsouth.com
www.rainbowfish.us
Meet Marcus Pfister at www.marcuspfister.ch

Marcus Pfister

Franz-Ferdinand
the Dancing Walrus

Translated by David Henry Wilson

North South

Franz-Ferdinand the walrus lay on his rock. He was a great big walrus, now forty-two years old, with two tusks that were more than three feet long. He weighed well over a ton, and if there was one thing Franz-Ferdinand hated, it was moving.

Walruses had to fight to have their own rock. And during his long life, Franz-Ferdinand had spent plenty of time fighting. His huge tusks had proved to be very useful, and his opponents had gone away with lots of scratches.

Franz-Ferdinand's favorite way to spend the day was watching the flamingos ballet dancing. In every respect they were the exact opposite of him. Perhaps that was the reason he was so fascinated.

Now you might wonder what flamingos were doing on the east coast of Greenland (where the walrus lived). Perhaps it was because the glaciers were melting. Or maybe it simply got too hot for them in Africa. But the flamingos were here, and that's all you need to know.

This was not any old flamingo ballet company. No, this was one of the most famous flamingo ballet schools in the world, under the direction of the now-somewhat-past-her-prime Madame Flamenco. She ran the company with an iron wing and had developed a completely new style of dance. This was not entirely a matter of choice. The fact was that if the flamingos stayed on the same spot for longer than two seconds, their feet got stuck to the icy surface. This problem resulted in their rather special and highly original form of ballet.

Franz-Ferdinand loved to watch these graceful creatures gliding smoothly over the ice. It was the first time in many years that he saw movement as something fascinatingly beautiful. And although it was true that he had now reached a certain age, everyone knows that nobody is ever too old to learn.

"Wow, I'd really like to try that myself," thought Franz-Ferdinand. He studied the movements of the ballet dancers and then secretly began to practice them himself.

Fortunately, his rock was some distance away from the rest of the walrus colony. He would have collapsed with embarrassment if any of his walrus friends had seen him ballet dancing.

At first he found it very frustrating, but with a good deal of self-discipline he worked on his weaknesses and made progress every day. After weeks of hard work, he felt fit and ready to put his great idea into practice. He set off to approach Madame Flamenco and her ballet dancers and ask if he could join her school. Inch by inch he dragged himself over the rocks, took his courage in both flippers, and introduced himself to her.

Madame Flamenco's greeting was not exactly the warmest of welcomes. The longer she listened, the wider went her eyes, and for a moment she even forgot to close her beak.

"Most worshipful madame, I am a great admirer of your art. I am fully aware that you will regard my physical qualifications for ballet dancing with a critical eye. Nevertheless, I would like to join your ballet classes."

Madame Flamenco tried to keep a straight face. However, she admired the courage and self-confidence of the giant pinniped, and she also wondered what he might do if she were to reject his application. His tusks were so powerful looking. Impressed by the cultured tone with which he had spoken to her, she said, "I will offer you one lesson, as a test." The lesson would take place there and then.

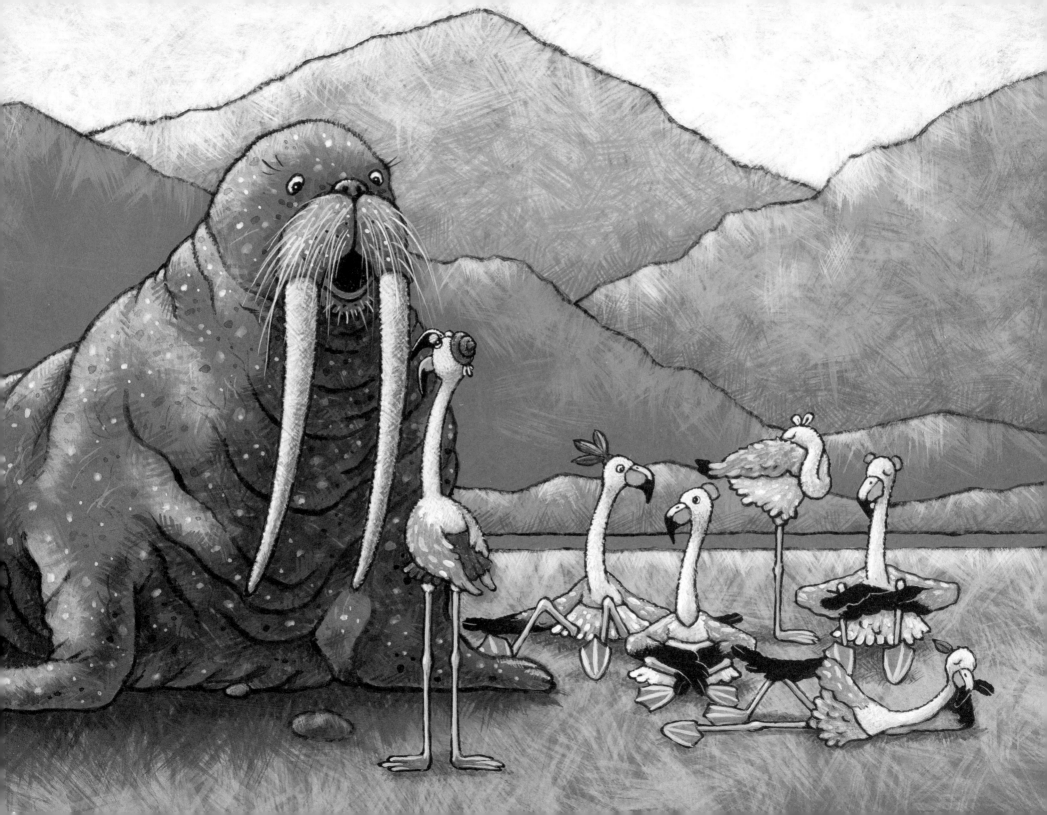

"I'll give you an audition," said Madame Flamenco, "but there's no way you can dance with us stark naked!"

Of course Franz-Ferdinand agreed, and so they started to look around for a suitable piece of clothing.

The feathered dresses of the flamingos looked very elegant and feminine — much too feminine for an overgrown walrus bull. A simple pair of swimming trunks would have to do. But where on the east coast of Greenland could a walrus find a pair of swimming trunks? The classy flamingos had brought outfits with them from Paris, but no matter how much he loved ballet, that was just a bit too far away for Franz-Ferdinand. And so he swam the short distance out to sea, as far as the nearest floating carpet of plastic garbage, and hunted around.

He saw plastic bottles and bags, coffee cups, drinking straws, and all kinds of plastic packets and containers—rubbish and more rubbish, as far as the eye could see! Disgusting! Who could have tipped all this garbage into the sea? However, the one thing he couldn't find was a pair of swimming trunks, and so he had to look for a new idea. He quickly grabbed a few plastic bottles and other bits and pieces, and bound them together on a plastic rope to tie around his big fat tummy. At last he had his tutu, and after a few attempts in the water, he succeeded in putting it on.

The tutu was not a pretty sight, but it served its purpose. Franz-Ferdinand wobbled back as fast as he could and arrived — puffing and blowing — just in time to take his place in the group.

And then the miracle happened. With unexpected grace and in defiance of all the laws of gravity, Franz-Ferdinand heaved himself upright, balanced himself on his tail fin, and began to dance lightly and smoothly over the ice. He already knew all the steps and all the different parts of the dancing lesson because he had watched the group so many times. Soon he seemed to be perfectly in harmony with all the flamingos, and at the same time he even learned some French. Croisé, glissé, jeté, plié, sauté; and finally of course he performed a perfect pirouette.

Madame Flamenco couldn't believe her eyes. She was enchanted by this superb natural talent and began to flap her wings with excitement. And when Franz-Ferdinand danced up to her and gallantly blew a kiss toward her wings (he knew he mustn't let his lips touch them, although he couldn't stop the extra-long hairs of his beard from lightly brushing her feathers), her heart was lost forever. She blushed and fell madly in love with her new star performer.

Madame Flamenco said, "Franz-Ferdinand, you are welcome to join our ballet school!"

But not everyone agreed with this decision. Some of the flamingos were afraid of the giant, and many of them had to be accompanied to the lessons by their parents. They were totally opposed to having a walrus at the ballet school. It was far too dangerous! And as for the tutu made of trash, ugh, it was disgusting! And so in the end, the parents decided they would hire a new teacher. Franz-Ferdinand and Madame Flamenco both had to leave. They were inconsolable.

Madame Flamenco had devoted her whole life to ballet, and now it was all over. Franz-Ferdinand did everything he could to cheer her up—but without success. Then suddenly he had an idea. "Madame Flamenco," he said. "It's true you don't have a ballet school anymore, but it would be a crying shame for you to waste your unique talents as a ballet teacher. We shall simply start a ballet school for walruses. I'll take care of the students, and you'll run the school. How about it?"

Madame Flamenco thought for a minute. A walrus ballet school could hardly be compared to a flamingo ballet school, but bearing in mind Franz-Ferdinand's extraordinary talent, it still sounded very promising.

"Thank you, Franz-Ferdinand. It's worth a try. By the way, please call me Amélie."

Franz-Ferdinand set to work at once. It was not for nothing that he was the head bull of the walrus herd. Everyone respected him. After a short but intensive recruitment campaign, he had managed to persuade five walruses to sign up. The five were told to swim out to the plastic garbage dump, put together their tutus, and attend their first lesson the next morning at 10:00 a.m. That gave them a whole day to get themselves fully motivated.

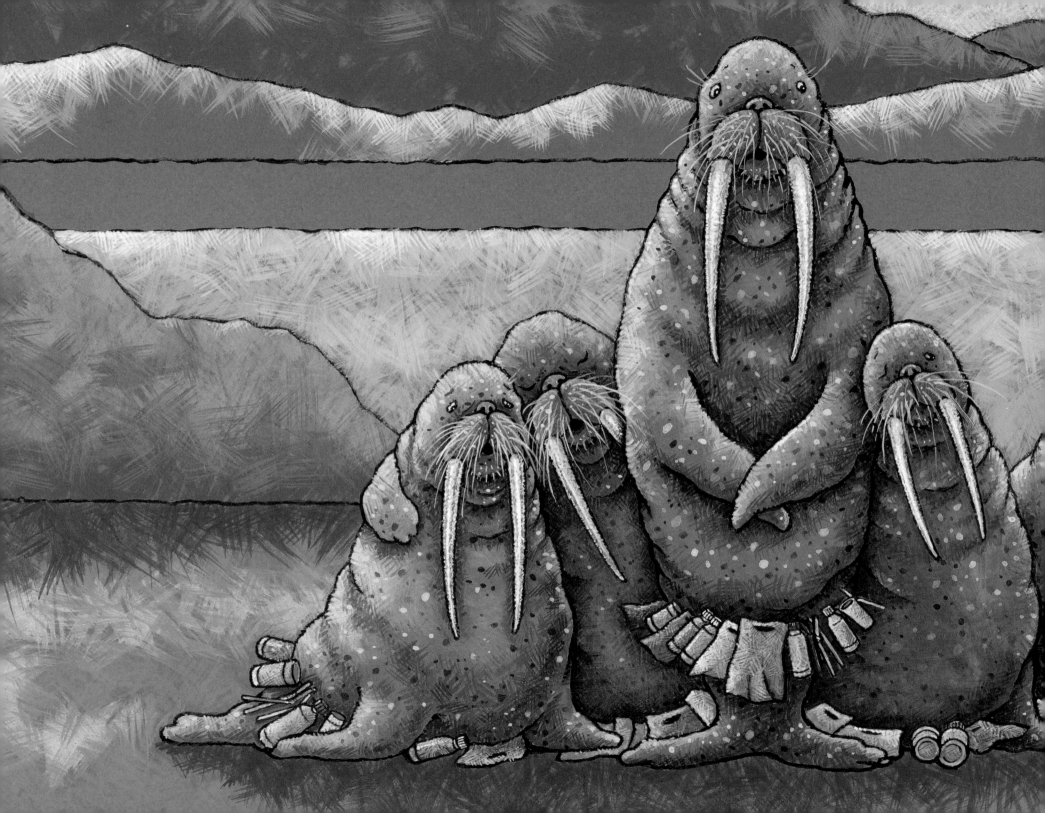

The next morning, Amélie took one look at her five new students, and her enthusiasm began to disappear. What had she been thinking of when she'd agreed to Franz-Ferdinand's suggestion? Oh well, at least she wouldn't have to spend the day twiddling her wings. She stood up straight and tall and addressed the class.

"Good morning, all of you. The first thing we need to do is work on your posture. Stand up straight and tall."

The walruses had been looking forward to a nice relaxing morning with just a few stretching exercises. They certainly hadn't expected this tough talk from the delicate-looking flamingo teacher.

Amazingly, though, after just a few weeks, all their hard work brought its reward, and the reluctant class of unwilling walruses had turned into really good dancers. Franz-Ferdinand was proud of Amélie. Amélie was proud of her new ballet company, and they both lived happily ever after. And the Walrus Ballet Company became the best—in fact, the only—walrus ballet company in the world.

Dear reader,

The walrus ballet students were happy to make their tutus out of the trash floating in the ocean, but most animals and humans are extremely unhappy about the enormous amount of garbage they find there. The great Pacific garbage patch, for instance, is about seven times the size of the United Kingdom or about the same size as California. Throwing trash into the ocean is not only pointless but also very dangerous both for animals and humans. The fact is that in time the plastic will disintegrate into tiny pieces, which will end up in the bodies of sea creatures and, eventually, in all of our bodies. This is bad for everyone.

Fortunately, though, just as walruses can learn to dance, all of us can learn new things. And so we humans can and must learn to change the wasteful and damaging habits of our consumer society.